what is happening
in the pictures.

Each child is an
individual and
develops at his
own pace.
Be patient
if your child
is struggling
with words.
It is more
important
to value what
he *can* do than to
become anxious about
progress. The learning
steps will all be taken in time, with your
help. At the back of this book you will find
suggestions on how to make the
best and fullest use of
this book.

---

* In order to avoid the clumsy 'he/she', the child is referred to as 'he'.

Geraldine Taylor is a national broadcaster, writer and authority on involving parents in their children's education. She contributes on this subject regularly to magazines for parents.

Working with schools in Avon, Geraldine helps parents and teachers to act in partnership to benefit children's learning confidence and family happiness.

Acknowledgment:
Front endpaper and cover illustrations by Lynn Breeze.

British Library Cataloguing in Publication Data
Taylor, Geraldine
    Talkabout shopping.
    1. English language. Readers—For pre-school children
    I. Title   II. Trotter, Stuart   III. Series
    428.6
    ISBN 0-7214-1120-7

Published by Ladybird Books Ltd Loughborough Leicestershire UK
Ladybird Books Inc Auburn Maine 04210 USA
© LADYBIRD BOOKS LTD MCMLXXXIX
Printed in England

talkabout

shopping

written by GERALDINE TAYLOR
illustrated by STUART TROTTER

Ladybird Books

Let's go shopping!

Which shop sells these?

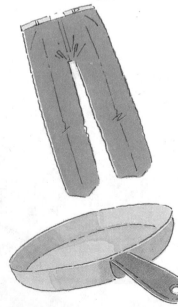

What do you think will happen next?

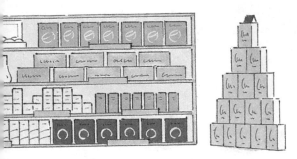

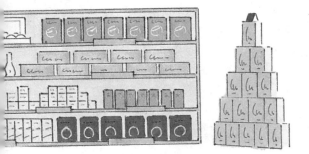

9

What's happening here?

Cobbler, cobbler, mend my shoe,
Get it done by half past two.
My toe is peeping through,
Cobbler, cobbler, mend my shoe.

Careful with the eggs!

Higgledy Piggledy, my black hen,
She lays eggs for gentlemen;
Sometimes nine and sometimes ten,
Higgledy Piggledy, my black hen.

Look at all the bread.
Which shapes do you like best?

Do you know this rhyme?

Four currant buns in a baker's shop,
Round and fat with sugar on top.
Along came a boy with a penny one day,
Bought a currant bun and took it away.

New shoes...

New coat...

New book...

New room...

See if you can find another like this:

and this:

and this.

17

What do these shops sell?

What's happening here?

Rain, rain go away —
Come again another day.

20

Rain, rain go away —
Don't come down on shopping day.

21

Tell the story.

Look at all the colours!

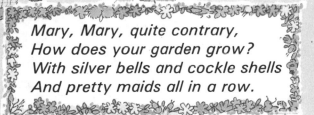

Mary, Mary, quite contrary,
How does your garden grow?
With silver bells and cockle shells
And pretty maids all in a row.

Let's look round the toy shop.

How many?

Can you find them in the pet shop?

Look out for these when you go shopping.

Time for something to eat!

To market, to market,
To buy a plum bun.
Home again, home again,
Market is done.

35

What's happening in the picture?

What happens next?

This shop sells all kinds of things.

What can you see?

Let's play shopping.

43

talkabout

talkabout shopping

Young children respond to the enthusiasm parents bring to discussions. If you are eager to talk and listen, your child will be, too. Don't feel self-conscious about bringing that all important excitement and fantasy to conversations with your child.

Ladybird talkabout books are designed to encourage children to talk about their everyday experiences. There are suggestions on each page which will help you and your child to talk imaginatively about shopping.

Going shopping is an adventure for children, an exciting landmark in their day or week. A child's-eye view of a shop is very vivid as there's so much to see and do.

Choosing fascinates children and **talkabout shopping** encourages discussion about which items we need and choose.